D1029490

Published by Familius™ LLC, www.familius.com
PO Box 1249 Reedley, Ca 93654.

Familius books are available at special discounts for bulk purchases, whether for sales promotions or for family or corporate use. For more information, email orders@familius.com.

Library of Congress Control Number: 2021938973
ISBN 9781641705691

Printed in China
Edited by Maggie Wickes and Brooke Jorden
Book and jacket design by Carlos Guerrero.

Images sourced or licensed from Shutterstock.

10 9 8 7 6 5 4 3 2 1

First Edition

12 Little Elves visit MISSOURI

by ANN INGALLS

ILLUSTRATIONS BY
VALERIA DANILOVA

FAMILIUS

'Twas Christmas in Missouri
and 12 elves were sent
to see who was sleeping . . .

. . . away the elves went!

In each home was nestled
each girl and each boy,
while visions of Missouri
brought everyone joy.

So curious now,
to the Plaza they sprinted.
The glow of the lights was
so bright that they squinted.

UNION STATION

A caboose, some boxcars,
and Santa's great sleigh
Union Station so festively
put on display.

The elves sipped hot cocoa
and ate Christmas treats
as they scurried down
St. Charles' cobblestone streets.

A million lights shone
in a shimmery show
at the vast Missouri
Botanical Garden Glow.

FOREST PARK TROLLEY

RK TROLLEY
M PARK
TROLLEY
As they rode in a bus
at the St. Louis Zoo,
there were reindeer to see
and dear Santa Claus too.

At Sycamore Creek,
the elves celebrated yuletide
with bonfires, s'mores,
and the Jingle Bell hayride.

Then the elves stopped in Branson
for toe-tapping shows!
There were holiday trees
decked with bells and bright bows.

Chateau on the Lake
had a fancy display
of gingerbread houses
and candy chalets.

The elves rode in carriages
in Sainte Genevieve
and sang joyful carols
that cold Christmas Eve.

A bundle of ribbons
and green mistletoe,
a kiss at the Gazebo,
and then, time to go.

Good night, Missouri.
You're all fast asleep,
but there's just one more house
that the elves want to see . . .

Hurry to bed
and shut your eyes tight.
Merry Christmas, dear Missouri.
12 elves say good night!